# DRAWING OUTDOORS

Jairo Buitrago + Rafael Yockteng

TRANSLATED BY Elisa Amado

AN ALDANA LIBROS BOOK

GREYSTONE KIDS

GREYSTONE BOOKS • VANCOUVER/BERKELEY/LONDON

Our school has almost nothing. A blackboard, some chairs.

It has a teacher. She's always there. She stands in the doorway and waits for us every morning.

For those who don't know how to get here, I can explain where it is.

My school is between two mountains,

near a river,

in the middle of nowhere.

Today the teacher tells us that our lessons will be outside.

We are explorers, we have paper, we have crayons.

Even the two boys who are twins and walk a very long way to get here, although they don't like school, want to come and draw outdoors with us.

"Look! Over there by the river, there's a Brontosaurus,"
says the teacher. "Let's all observe it very closely."

"There it is!"

"Yes. There it is!"

"Look. Over there! On that big rock, there's a Triceratops,"
says the teacher.

"Triceratops!"

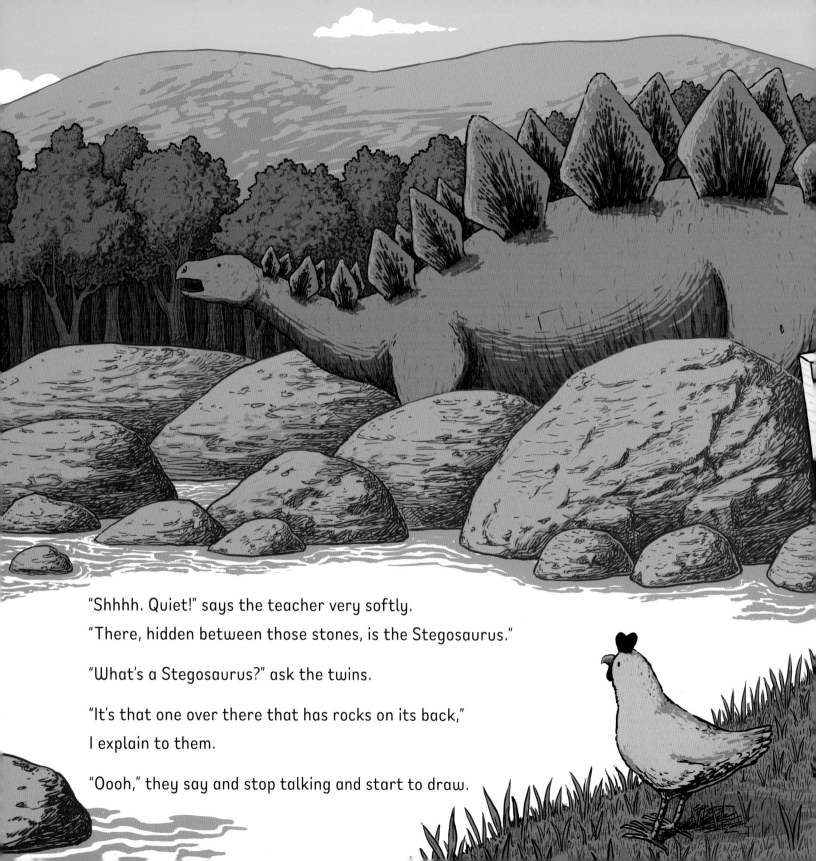

"Shhhh. Quiet!" says the teacher very softly.

"There, hidden between those stones, is the Stegosaurus."

"What's a Stegosaurus?" ask the twins.

"It's that one over there that has rocks on its back,"
I explain to them.

"Oooh," they say and stop talking and start to draw.

Suddenly the sky grows dark.

"What's that?"

"Is a storm coming, teacher?"

"No! Look. Up there! Pterodactyls are covering the sun."

Suddenly a wind picks up that blows the trees.
The mountain booms and the birds stop singing.

"Don't make a sound, it's dangerous," the teacher says.

We crouch down carefully and keep peering into the woods.

"There," says Juana.

It's roaring among the trees! A Tyrannosaurus rex!

Some of us run back to the school.

Only the bravest of us stay on and draw.

Then we sit on a branch as big as an Ankylosaurus to eat our snacks.

And we see a squirrel.

When it's time to go home, I have lots of drawings.
I'm tired and my cheeks are red. The teacher says
goodbye to me. She's standing in the doorway.

On the path, I look back and see my school.

My school has almost nothing. A blackboard, some chairs.

And it has a teacher, and a Brontosaurus that's as big as a mountain.

**For my nieces and nephews**
**from whom I learn every day —R.Y.**

22 23 24 25 26  5 4 3 2 1

Greystone Kids / Greystone Books Ltd.
greystonebooks.com

An Aldana Libros book

Cataloguing data available from Library and Archives Canada
ISBN 978-1-77164-847-9 (cloth)
ISBN 978-1-77164-848-6 (epub)

FSC
www.fsc.org
MIX
Paper from
responsible sources
FSC® C016973

Jacket and text design by Sara Gillingham Studio
Printed and bound in Singapore on FSC® certified paper at COS Printers Pte Ltd.
The FSC® label means that materials used for the product have been responsibly sourced.
The illustrations in this book were rendered digitally.

Greystone Books gratefully acknowledges the Musqueam, Squamish, and Tsleil-Waututh
peoples on whose land our Vancouver head office is located.

Greystone Books thanks the Canada Council for the Arts, the British Columbia Arts Council,
the Province of British Columbia through the Book Publishing Tax Credit, and the Government
of Canada for supporting our publishing activities.

Canada

Canada Council
for the Arts
Conseil des arts
du Canada

BRITISH
COLUMBIA

BRITISH COLUMBIA
ARTS COUNCIL
An agency of the Province of British Columbia